D

# Case of the
# MISSING
# DINOSAUR

Written by Keith Brandt
Illustrated by John Wallner

## Troll Associates

*Library of Congress Cataloging in Publication Data*

Brandt, Keith (date).
   Case of the missing dinosaur.

   (A Troll easy-to-read mystery)
   Summary: Twins Karen and Kathy try to find out
what happened to Irving the dinosaur, their base-
ball team mascot.
   [1. Mystery and detective stories.  2. Dinosaurs
—Fiction.  3. Baseball—Fiction]  I. Wallner,
John C., ill.  II. Title.  III. Series: Troll easy-
to-read mystery.
PZ7.B73733Cas    [Fic]    81-7620
ISBN 0-89375-586-9 (case)    AACR2
ISBN 0-89375-587-7 (pbk.)

10   9   8   7   6   5   4   3   2   1

# Case of the
# MISSING
# DINOSAUR

Everything was going great for the Blue Jays. That's our baseball team. My name is Josh. I'm the catcher.

Andy was pitching better than ever. And Peggy, our best slugger, hit a streak of homers. We were in first place.

We were playing well, for sure. But that's not all. We were lucky, too. That's because we had Irving. Irving is the team mascot. Irving is also a dinosaur. He cheers for us at every game. He wears a Blue Jay cap. He dusts off the bases with his tail. He puts the numbers on the scoreboard.

Irving is always happy. He makes us feel good. Every team needs a mascot, and Irving is ours.

Irving lives in a barn behind Kathy and Karen's house. Kathy and Karen are twins. Kathy plays first base. Karen plays second base. Or maybe it's the other way—Karen on first and Kathy on second. I can never tell them apart. But Irving can.

Irving is a true friend. When our kites get stuck in a tree, he brings them down. On Halloween, he gets lots of candy. People never say no to a dinosaur as high as their house.

Irving is very gentle, too. He gives rides to everybody. All you have to do is get on his back and say, "Giddyup!" And away he goes.

Before every game the team meets at Irving's barn. He makes sure we're ready to play ball. One time Nancy forgot her Blue Jay cap. Irving let her wear his cap. Then Irving found a straw hat in the barn. He wore that—with a blue and white ribbon on it. Those are our team colors.

It was the afternoon of a big game. The Blue Jays against the Hawks. I was on my way to Irving's barn.

On the way, I met Bob and Nancy and Steve. They are Blue Jays. They play in the outfield. They're always together off the field, too.

"Hi, guys," I said. "What's new?"

"We were out—" said Bob.

"At the field, playing—" said Nancy.

"Catch," said Steve.

"It won't be easy—" said Bob.

"To beat the—" said Nancy.

"Hawks," said Steve.

They always talk that way. From left to right.

We got to where the twins live. We walked across the back yard to the barn. Nobody was there. The doors were wide open.

"Irving," I called.

"Get—" said Bob.

"Your Blue Jay—" said Nancy.

"Cap," said Steve.

There was silence.

"I guess Irving is out picking flowers in the field," I said.

The three outfielders agreed.

"Let's sit—" said Bob.

"Down and—" said Nancy.

"Wait," said Steve.

A minute later Peggy got there. Then
Andy. And Rick. We waited and waited.
Bob, Nancy, and Steve played catch. Andy
made believe he was pitching.

"I wish Karen and Kathy would get
here," Rick said.

"Yes, and Irving," Peggy said.

"It's getting late. It's almost time to
go," said Andy.

Just then the twins came racing
around the barn. They looked scared.

"What happened?" I asked.

"Irving is gone!" wailed Karen.

"We were bringing him lunch," said Kathy. "He always eats twelve peanut-butter-and-jelly sandwiches. And a gallon of chocolate milk. He loves sweet things." She began to cry.

"And he wasn't in the barn?" I asked. "Or picking flowers?"

The unhappy twins shook their heads.

"Maybe he wasn't hungry," Rick said.

"Maybe he went to the baseball field," Peggy said.

Kathy stopped crying. "We didn't look there," she said.

Karen grabbed Irving's big lunch basket. Bob, Nancy, and Steve grabbed the bats and balls. I got Irving's Blue Jay cap.

We all hurried to the ball field.

Irving wasn't there. But the Hawks were. And they were ready to play.

"Come on, Blue Jays," said the Hawks' pitcher. "Let's start the game."

"Not yet," I said. "Irving isn't here."

"Who's Irving?" asked the Hawks' catcher.

"He's their dopey dinosaur," the pitcher told him.

"Irving is not dopey!" Peggy yelled. "He's the smartest, bravest, kindest dinosaur in the whole world."

"And he brings us good luck," said Andy.

We waited for five minutes. Still no Irving. We had to start the game without him.

The Blue Jays were awful. Peggy didn't get one hit. Nobody else did, either. Except the Hawks. They slugged Andy's pitches all over the field.

There was nobody to cheer for us, and nobody to put the numbers on the scoreboard. Anyway, we lost: 37–0.

We played the Robins the next day.
Without Irving. And the Blue Jays were
really bad again. We made ten errors.

We lost this game 26–0.

After the game we sat on the bench.
We all felt gloomy.

Peggy banged her bat on the ground. "We need our mascot," she said. "We can't win without him."

"I miss him," said Kathy.

"So do I," said Karen.

"I think he got lost," said Rick.

"I bet—" said Bob.

"Irving was—" said Nancy.

"Kidnapped," said Steve.

I jumped to my feet. "Well, we must find him," I said.

"Irving is big. It's hard to hide him,"
said Andy.

Rick took out a pencil and a piece of
paper. "I'll make a list. We'll call it —
PLACES TO HUNT FOR IRVING."

We named all the places where you
could find a dinosaur. Rick put them on
the list.

"We'll meet here tomorrow morning
to start the hunt," I said. "Okay?"

Everybody agreed.

And we all went home.

The first place on our list was the museum. It was huge. We did not know where to look first.

A guard came over to us. "Can I help you?" he asked.

"Do you have a dinosaur here?" Karen asked him.

"Yes, we do. Up on the second floor," the guard said.

"Is his name Irving?" Rick asked.

The guard rubbed his head. "I don't know his name. But it's printed on a white card upstairs," he said.

"Thank you," I said.

"Let's go, gang!" said Peggy.

We ran up the big marble stairs. Past the Hall of Rocks. Past the Hall of Clocks. Through the Indian Village. Into the Den of Dinosaurs.

We found six dinosaurs. But not one of them was Irving.

We left the museum. We went to the big toy store.

Then we went to the chocolate factory, the roller-skating rink, the beach, and the playgrounds.

No Irving.

"Maybe we will find him at the zoo,"
said Peggy.

"Yes, Irving loves animals," said
Kathy—or Karen.

We walked through the park and
followed the signs that said TO THE ZOO.

Suddenly, Andy yelled, "Look! I see
Irving!"

Andy ran. We followed him. He ran
past the bears. Past the tigers. Past the
elephants. And monkeys. And seals.

Then he stopped. So did we.

"That's—" said Bob.

"Not—" said Nancy.

"Irving," said Steve.

The animal was tall. And it had a long neck. But it wasn't a dinosaur.

"Boy, am I dumb," Andy groaned.

"Well," said Karen, "from far away a giraffe does sort of look like a dinosaur."

"Sure," said Kathy. "Are there any more places on our list?"

Rick held up the piece of paper. "Just the police station," he said.

And off we went.

A police officer sat behind a high desk at the station house.

"I'm Officer Black. Can I help you?" he asked.

"Irving is missing," I said.

"Could you tell me what he looks like?" asked Officer Black.

"He's tall as a tree," said Bob.

"His skin is green," said Nancy.

"And he has a long tail with a curl at the end of it," said Steve.

Officer Black's eyes opened wide. So did his mouth.

"Jones," Officer Black called out.

Another officer came over. Officer Black told her, "You take care of this."

Officer Jones was nice. She listened to our story about Irving.

"I think he was kidnapped," Peggy said.

"So do we," said Kathy and Karen.

"I think somebody hid him," said Rick.

"I am sure he would come home if he could," I said.

"Please put out a missing person—I mean, a missing dinosaur report," begged Andy.

Officer Jones smiled. "I think we can crack this case right now," she said.

"Come with me," Officer Jones said. We followed her outside and went down the street. She stopped at a fence. There was a big sign on it. The sign said:

SAMMY'S CIRCUS PRESENTS
DANDY THE DYNAMITE DINO!!

Right under the words there were pictures of Irving. In one picture, he was walking on a wire way above the ground. In another picture, a lot of little kids were sliding down his neck. In another, he had a saddle on his back. He was giving a ride to a boy and girl.

"I'll take you there now," Officer
Jones said.

We all piled into a police car for the
ride to Sammy's Circus.

There were tents and rides and games
to play. There were people selling peanuts
and popcorn and cotton candy. We heard
music and laughing. Everybody was
having great fun.

"There's Sammy. You can ask him about Irving," said Officer Jones.

Sammy was short and fat. He was wearing a jacket with green and white stripes. His pants had blue and red checks. His tie was yellow with purple polka dots. On one hand, he wore a sparkling diamond ring.

"Mister Sammy," I said. "We came for our dinosaur."

"You mean my star, Dandy?" Sammy asked.

"His name is Irving, sir. And we need him," Peggy said.

"I need him, too," Sammy said. "The circus needs him. The whole world needs him!"

Suddenly, there was a loud squeal. We all turned around. It was Irving, running over to see us. He kissed all the Blue Jays.

He hopped up and down. He waved his
tail like a flag. Irving was as excited as
could be. So were we.

"Come on, Irving. Let's go home,"
said Karen.

"Wait a second," said Sammy.
"Maybe Irving wants to stay with me." He
was holding four huge cones of pink
cotton candy.

Irving looked at the cotton candy.
Then he looked at us. Then at the candy.
Then at us. Irving didn't know what to do.

"So!" shouted Karen, pointing at Sammy. "You kidnapped Irving with cotton candy!"

Sammy looked sorry. "I saw the big guy picking flowers in a field," he said. "I just wanted to make him a star."

First, Sammy promised Irving lots of money. Irving didn't want money. Then Sammy promised him all the cotton candy he could eat. That did it.

"And you gave him cotton candy to keep him here," said Officer Jones. "That is not nice."

Sammy hung his head.

"Wait. I have an idea," said Rick.
"You know, some days we don't play
baseball."

"Right! And Irving can come here on
those days," Peggy said.

"And be your star," I said.
"And eat—" said Bob.
"Lots of—" said Nancy.
"Cotton candy," said Steve.

"Then he can come home and sleep in his own barn," said Kathy.

Sammy and Officer Jones smiled. Everyone, including Irving, was very happy.

With our mascot back, the Blue Jays won every game. And the championship.

Sammy threw a big party for us.
There were clowns and animals and
acrobats and the circus band. And a tub
full of cotton candy for the star of the
show—Irving.